For my agent, Kathleen Rushall—I tried to think of a clever dedication,
and I wanted it to be a surprise, but to keep it a surprise I couldn't run it by you, so now
I fear this is a pretty terrible dedication and also very likely a run-on sentence. . . .
Also, thanks for everything. - J. F.

For my lovely family. Thank you. - E. G.

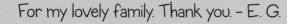

STERLING CHILDREN'S BOOKS
New York

An Imprint of Sterling Publishing Co., Inc.
1166 Avenue of the Americas
New York, NY 10036

ISBN 978-1-4549-2258-2

Distributed in Canada by Sterling Publishing Co., Inc.
c/o Canadian Manda Group, 664 Annette Street
Toronto, Ontario, M6S 2C8, Canada
Distributed in the United Kingdom by GMC Distribution Services
Castle Place, 166 High Street, Lewes, East Sussex, BN7 1XU, England
Distributed in Australia by NewSouth Books
45 Beach Street, Coogee, NSW 2034, Australia

For information about custom editions, special sales, and premium and corporate purchases,
please contact Sterling Special Sales at 800-805-5489 or specialsales@sterlingpublishing.com.

Manufactured in China

Lot #:
2 4 6 8 10 9 7 5 3 1
02/18

sterlingpublishing.com

Cover and interior design by Heather Kelly
The artwork for this book was created digitally.

ALBIE NEWTON

BY JOSH FUNK

ILLUSTRATED BY ESTER GARAY

STERLING CHILDREN'S BOOKS
New York

Little Albie Newton
was a thinker from the start.

He built a mega-stroller
after taking his apart.

The day that Albie learned to count,
he ran to Mom and cried.

He couldn't reach infinity,
despite how hard he tried.

Albie moved to Littleton and joined a class midyear.
The children welcomed Albie when they sang their morning cheer:

"Clap your hands, good morning! It's great today's today!
Here at school you'll make some friends, discover, learn, and play!"

γειά σου

HELLO

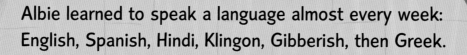

Albie learned to speak a language almost every week:
English, Spanish, Hindi, Klingon, Gibberish, then Greek.

Albie started formulating plans to make some friends.
I'll construct a special gift before the school day ends.

Very soon the students noticed Albie was a whiz.

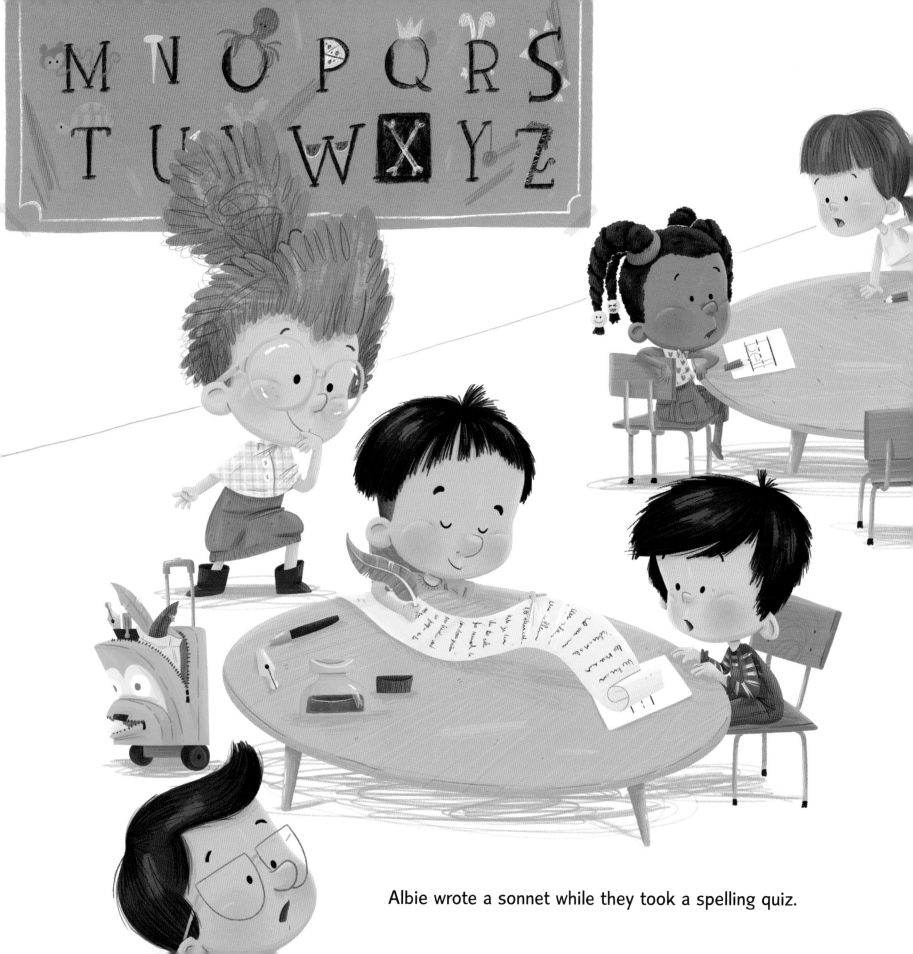

Albie wrote a sonnet while they took a spelling quiz.

Shirley painted lots of swirly circles in a row.
Albie painted starry nights on canvas like van Gogh.

Kai and Jane played dress-up
till they heard a giant. . .

CRASH!

Albie dumped the garbage bin
and sifted through the trash.

Arjun ate his snack and finished Albie's cleanup duties
as Albie built a science lab (and found a cure for cooties!).

Hamilton the hamster tried to run but had no wheel.

Albie needed extra sprockets made of stainless steel.

Sona couldn't find the glue to finish up her mask.

Albie swiped the whole supply and didn't even ask.

Dave propelled a wind-up plane across the classroom rug.
Albie picked it up and pulled its wings off with a tug.

Evie tried to read a book with Adra and Raúl as

BOOMING PANDEMONIUM

descended on the school.

But Albie didn't notice all the problems he was causing.
Focused on important things, he never thought of pausing.

An angry mob of children rumbled through the classroom rubble.
"Wait a minute," Shirley said. "I know he caused us trouble!"

But maybe Albie didn't know. Let's look at what he made."
Curious, the children headed straight to where he played.

Everybody gawked at Albie's mountain of inventions.

Could it be that Albie Newton had no bad intentions?

The kids agreed the spaceship was the best they'd ever seen.

"Spaceship . . ." Albie pushed a button.

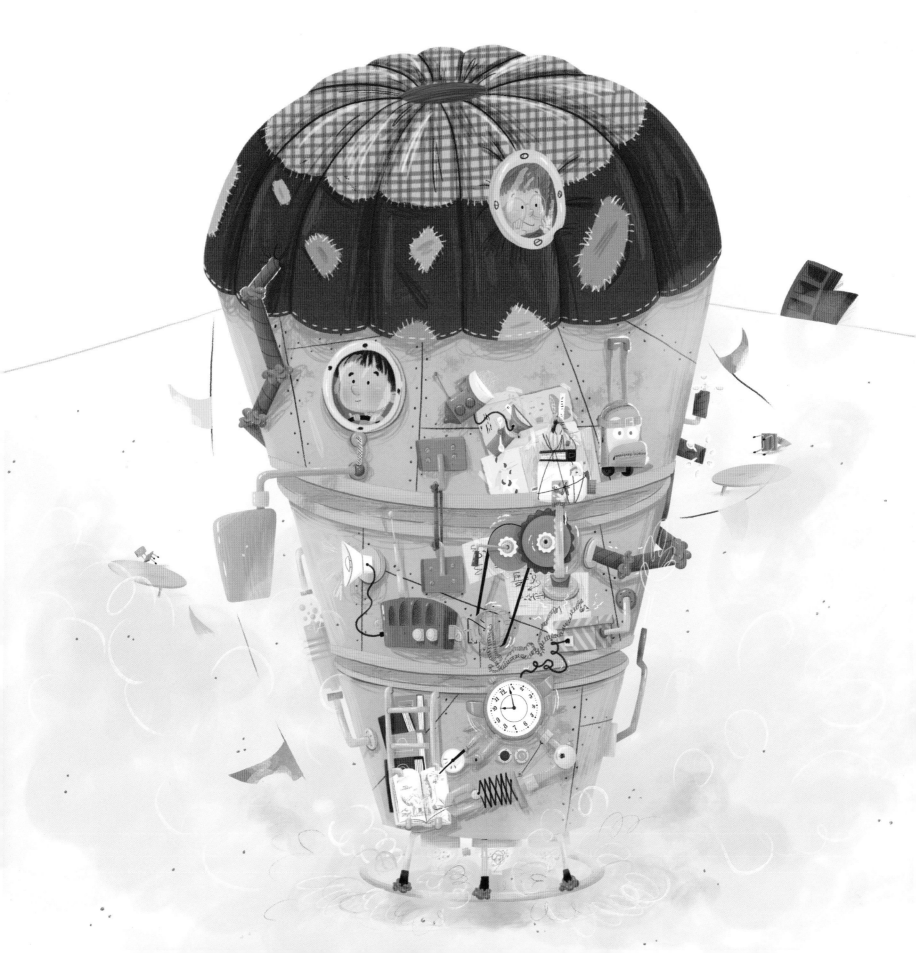

"... and a time machine!"